The Green Orb
of Boltonia

Lisa A. Biczi

iUniverse, Inc.
Bloomington

The Green Orb of Boltonia

This is a work of fiction. All of the characters, names, incidents, organizations, and dialogue in this novel are either the products of the author's imagination or are used fictitiously.

iUniverse books may be ordered through booksellers or by contacting:

iUniverse
1663 Liberty Drive
Bloomington, IN 47403
www.iuniverse.com
1-800-Authors (1-800-288-4677)

Because of the dynamic nature of the Internet, any web addresses or links contained in this book may have changed since publication and may no longer be valid. The views expressed in this work are solely those of the author and do not necessarily reflect the views of the publisher, and the publisher hereby disclaims any responsibility for them.

Any people depicted in stock imagery provided by Thinkstock are models, and such images are being used for illustrative purposes only.

Certain stock imagery © Thinkstock.

ISBN: 978-1-4759-4109-8 (sc)
ISBN: 978-1-4759-4110-4 (e)

Library of Congress Control Number: 2012913553

Printed in the United States of America

iUniverse rev. date: 8/29/12

The wisest Elder has had a vision that a strong and powerful warrior will steal the Green Orb, the life force of the lands of Boltonia. The fate of the lands of Boltonia lies in the hands of a halfling, Merlinian, and the son of a union she will have with the thieving warrior. This is the prophecy.

Chapter 1
The Waiting

The green ivy grew up the outside wall of the small one-room cottage. It reached up onto the brown, dry thatched roof, where it tried to touch the last of the fall day's warm sun. A gentle breeze blew sand past the ivy and moved it slightly. The cottage sat lonesome in the dusty, dead valley. The grass around the cottage was lush and green. The leaves of a large, old oak tree that were once green slowly turned red as fall progressed. The smoke from the chimney seemed to call out for someone or something to notice the cottage from afar.

Inside the cottage, near a fireplace sat an old cotter, an old halfling creature from an Elfin mother and a human father. He had studied the old way of Merlin and was the greatest Merlinian in Boltonia. The glow of the firelight shimmered on a still face, which held the evidence of war in its cracks. He was missing his left eye, and his gray hair grew past his shoulders and was tucked behind his thin, pointed ears. His clothes, once of the finest silk, were tattered and musty. Still, this old cotter was neither neglected nor forgotten.

His furniture was worn by time and dried by the air yet still was comfortable and familiar and scattered around the room. A blanket of wool that had once been owned by the king now was moth-eaten. It lay neatly on the bed. The bed stood lonely and majestic in a corner distant from the other pieces of furniture. On the round table in center of the room was a small bowl of green apples piled high and a pitcher of sweet mead. His small feast was set for the guest for whom he waited.

His wait dragged on for days and nights. Still, he sat alone. Daily chores that passed the time would not make the time pass fast enough. It was time to bless the hearth. He grabbed the timeless broom that stood next to the fireplace, a cord, and a three-wick candle made especially for him by the elves of his homeland. It was stained with soot. He lit the wicks of the candle with an unsteady hand while chanting:

"I bring this home, I bring love to this home, and I bring honor to this home."

He tied a knot in the cord and then tied the cord to the broom. He swept the scanty cottage free of all its negative energies and feelings. Again he chanted.

"All that is evil is now swept away, and nothing but good shall come this way."

He could cleanse the hearth many times while he waited, but it would never cleanse the evil that would arrive.

He sat at the table to rest for a time after the cleansing. He watched the sun fall behind the White Mountains. The evening skies shone a dazzling array of pinks, reds, and violets. He became weary.

Suddenly, he sat up and strained as if he heard something. He smiled as soon as the sound became audible. It was the sound of charging horses headed toward the tiny cottage. He sat still for a moment, not out of fear but to prepare himself for his important guest. He heard them outside his door and moved only to pour two goblets of mead for him and his guest.

The door swung open and a tall, dark figure stood in the doorway.

"Come in. I've been expecting you, Barsabbas," the old cotter said without raising his head.

Barsabbas entered the cottage, his long emerald cloak dragging behind him. He was another halfling of a human mother and a giant father from the Forest of Shadows. His steps made slow, heavy thumps on the wooden floor. The firelight showed his face; it too had seen its share of battles and was weary. Barsabbas was tall and dark, but he had the brightest blue eyes.

"Emer, you old goat, I expected a better domicile. These are such humble means for such a great—"

"Don't say it, Barsabbas," Emer interrupted. "I'm no longer anyone's magikian."

"I'm not here to debate with you, old Elf. I'm here for your granddaughter."

"She is not here, as you can see," the cotter answered quickly.

"You know where she is. My men reported that she was living here with you, learning your ways."

"Your men are mistaken. I haven't seen Astarta in years, and teaching that child anything would be a feat of magik even *I* could not perform," Emer lied. He pushed the mead in front of Barsabbas and offered him a seat.

"Old elf, if I didn't fear you as I do, I would cut out your tongue and fry it up for dinner."

"The fear is only in your mind, Barsabbas. You know I can see inside you. I always could. I'm no one you should fear. We have been through much in these past years. Besides, I may be old, but I would have fought hard for my tongue before giving it up to the likes of you." He gave a good, hearty chuckle.

"Emer, your granddaughter took something that belongs to me. I need to know where she is," Barsabbas demanded as he slammed his closed fist on the table, spilling some of the mead from the goblets.

"The Green Orb was never yours. You stole it from the Elders, and this is what all this destruction and devastation is all about. We were warned about this. You are the cause of all this trouble over a worthless piece of rock."

"Ha. You do know where she is. You know as well as I that the Green Orb is no worthless piece of rock. Have you forgotten already?" Barsabbas looked up at the window and saw the ivy that was growing into the room. "I see you haven't forgotten how to use the orb. You know as well as me that whoever holds the orb will be all-powerful."

"So now, Barsabbas, you tell me you have no power. I doubt that very much. You control all these lands now that Viktor is dead. He was supposed to die, and you knew that. You have his armies of hundreds of men. For what? To chase down a girl with a rock? That seems like a waste of resources. But it is the girl you must fear. But you know that. That's right. I've warned you to stay away from her," Emer said sternly.

"You can think whatever you want, old elf, but I will have the girl and the orb. You *will* tell me where they are," Barsabbas demanded again. He took out his athame and twirled the point into the dry wood of the table.

"You know torture has never swayed me. I lost my eye to prove that."

"One thing I have to say for you, Emer, you're loyal. To torture you would truly be wasteful of my resources. Emer, I have something special for you, a reunion of sorts."

Barsabbas swiftly moved from his seat to the door, where he called for his men. Three soldiers entered the cottage.

"Take him," Barsabbas commanded, pointing at the old man.

Emer put up a struggle, but the soldiers were able to subdue him with great ease. He refused to use his magik. He let the soldiers take him. As they left the cottage, Barsabbas yelled to a few of the other men, commanding that the cottage and everything in it be burned.

"Where the old Elf is going now, he will no longer need any of these things. This will be a clear message to Astarta," Barsabbas said to his men. Then he climbed onto the back of his black stallion, Strength, who held still as Barsabbas seated himself comfortably. He commanded two soldiers to stand watch.

"You are to bring her to me when she is captured."

"What if she doesn't show?" the soldier asked.

"She'll show. I know her all too well. She'll show," Barsabbas confirmed. He waited on the back of Strength, watching as the cottage and its contents burned to the ground. Only after burnt rubble was all that was left did he turn Strength northward, leaving with his men and the old cotter.

The green ivy that had grown up to the thatch dried but did not burn as it fell to the ground in a small brown mass.

Chapter 2

The Charity

A young boy wore all black under an emerald-hooded cloak. He ran through the marketplace with a basket of fruits and bread that he had just stolen from the wealthy vendors of the market. A quite hefty vendor tried to keep up with the thief, but he was no match of the young boy's speed and agility. The boy pushed swiftly through the crowd as if he could fly. In the distance, the boy heard, "Stop, thief! He stole my fruit!"

These were wretched times in a kingdom without a king. The poor had dropped into the deepest poverty while the affluent fought for the throne of a kingdom that had been devastated by its own lands. The land, which had once been vibrant with colorful fruits, had become a vast wasteland with no growth and no food that could feed the hungry. Large stockpiles of food were used only for the wealthier inhabitants. The vendors had little defense against the hungry, thieves, and roustabouts common in the marketplace.

The whispers in the marketplace were that the cause of all their troubles was a theft of the Green Orb. Questions as to why and where were left unanswered. Whimsical stories came of it such as that the Green Orb was taken by King Viktor and was buried with him or a white-winged dragon flew off with it to a foreign land outside Boltonia. As the stories grew, there were still no answers, and the land continued to die around them.

The thief turned the corner, dropped the hood, and let out her long strawberry-blonde hair. Astarta belonged to the court of King Viktor; she was related to him through their mothers. She had been given every advantage of learning that a noble could have. She was learned in chemistry, alchemy, magik, the history of Boltonia and Merlin, disguise, fine arts, and theater. She was a small, agile, with a feature of her Elfin heritage, pointed ears. She had her mother's beautiful hair and snow white skin and her father's agility. Her eyes were almond shaped, brown in color but their color changed with her mood. She would have liked them to be a calm blue, but they were an anxious green at the moment. She walked slowly as the vendor rushed past her. She often disguised herself as a boy in the market to get what she needed for those who were less fortunate.

In these destitute times, even the wealthy had problems providing for themselves, but Astarta always gave her share and then some to the less fortunate. Astarta took her bounty to the orphanage so that the loving caregivers could feed the orphans. She rang the bell and waited. As she waited, she drifted into memory.

"Lady Astarta, you mustn't waste your time and money on those beggar children," her lady-in-waiting, Martha, an Elf, had said once as she helped her through the opened window. She was a small, round Elf with a bright face and a twinkle in her hazel eyes. She was dressed in a dark green gown with a white satin sash around her large waist. After Astarta climbed through the window, Martha quickly pulled the heavy drapes closed.

"But who will take care of them if I don't?" Astarta asked as she took off her emerald cape and shook away the snow that left a light dusting on the floor.

"The Elders will take care of them," her lady-in-waiting preached. She returned to her seat near the fireplace and continued with her needlework.

"I am just helping the Elders along," Astarta said as she moved gracefully to the fireplace and picked up her book of herbal remedies.

"If King Viktor finds out about your little excursions, he will have a watch on you all day and all night."

"What the king doesn't know won't hurt him. Besides, Viktor would encourage my generosity."

They sat quietly. Astarta put down her book and sat up straight in her chair as if she had heard something. She jumped out of her chair.

"He's here!"

"Who is here?"

A heavy knock came on the thick oak door of the bed chamber.

"Who is it?" the lady-in-waiting asked through the door.

"It's Barsabbas," Astarta answered.

"Barsabbas, General of Arms. I'm here to see Lady Astarta." The deep voice of the warrior was smooth.

"Oh, Martha, he's back, he's back," Astarta said. She was as excited as a child on Yule evening, viewing the beautiful festival of lights.

"Lady Astarta …" Martha said, trying to stop Astarta from running to the door. Then Martha slipped on her petticoat. Astarta opened the door, and in the doorway stood the tall and dark Barsabbas, General of Arms of all of King Viktor's armies. He entered the bed chamber and dragged his emerald cloak, dusted with snow, behind him.

"Leave us, Martha," Astarta instructed. Her eyes never left her handsome warrior. Martha left them. When the door was securely closed, she was finally alone with Barsabbas.

"How were the lands of Plumbaginium?" she asked. "I have never traveled that far south."

"I was there for battle, not a summer holiday. We fought hard, but we won the lands for Viktor, our king," he said. Then he settled himself on her bed.

"Oh, Barsabbas, that is wonderful. And you are home to me. I am so happy," she said. She moved to the bed and knelt to one side of him, removing his sandals and heavy woolen socks. She looked into his face and realized he was preoccupied. "Do you like my new gown?" she asked. "Viktor acquired it for me while he was in Verbena." She got up and twirled around. Barsabbas did not answer her. "Barsabbas, he is making you go into the highlands, isn't he?"

"I have to leave in the morning. I didn't want to tell you, but I had a feeling you already knew. The wedding is being postponed as we speak," Barsabbas said.

"Viktor knows the prophecy as well as any of us. He wants to prevent the inevitable," she said. She knelt again next to her warrior, placing her head in his lap. She felt him pet her strawberry-blonde hair with his large, muscular hand.

"Astarta, I know that one day you will destroy me, but I can't stay away from you. I will marry you with or without Viktor's blessing," Barsabbas admitted to her. He lifted her head, looked into her eyes, and kissed her passionately.

"Viktor is going to the Highlands with you," she said.

"What are you saying?"

"Not only is he postponing the wedding, but he is planning to travel to the Highlands tomorrow morning." She stared off as if she was listening to a sound far away. The scene was playing out right before her eyes.

She saw Viktor as he prepared for his journey. He advised his servants what to place in his travel satchel. He was a dazzling and fit, with stunning blond hair and green eyes. He too had the Elfin feature of pointed ears that his blond hair was tucked neatly behind. He turned and called out for Emer, but he was not there. Viktor shrugged off the notion that he would go into this battle without him. He had never gone into battle without his Merlinian grandfather.

Astarta was taken to an earlier moment when Viktor and Emer had argued.

"This is a very foolish journey, Viktor. I cannot advise you to go."

"Emer, Grandfather, my Merlinian, you know it is my time."

"Viktor, you leave us without a king. I will not be there to watch you leave us."

Viktor had stood before his grandfather proudly, with his head high.

"It is what has to be done. Do what you have to for Astarta, the new king, and Boltonia. That is what you need to do."

Viktor had hugged his grandfather and left the room.

"He doesn't trust me. Does he think I am inferior?" Barsabbas said in frustration, bringing Astarta back from her vision.

"No. He knows his end is near. Emer told him."

"Do you go into his mind?"

"I know I shouldn't, but it just comes to me like a dream."

"Then you know what is to come of us all."

"Yes, but it doesn't have to be that way. We could change it. Viktor is afraid to die. He knows that the Drummonds in the highlands will not end their quest for a realm of their own. Viktor is sorry for dissolving the Alliance and he prays to the Elders that, if he lives, the Alliance will be resurrected. Barsabbas, what is this alliance?"

"He speaks of this Alliance?"

"Only that if this alliance had not been dissolved the land would not be in turmoil. Oh, and the Green Orb."

"Astarta, I want you to take care of something for me." Barsabbas took from his cloak a ball of the brightest green. It made the entire chamber glow green.

"The Green Orb. I have studied its power. This is what Viktor is looking for," Astarta said quickly, her eyes open wide.

"This holds great powers. It holds the fate of the entire land of Boltonia.

Do not give this to Viktor. Do not give it to anyone. Keep it in a safe place. I will claim it when and if I return," he advised her as he handed the orb to her gingerly. She was amazed that she was holding the power source.

"How did you acquire this powerful orb?"

"I won it in a game of darts while I was traveling to Plumbaginium," he gave the lie he had prepared.

"You must know that I don't believe it," she said. She knew he had stolen it. In a vision, she watched Barsabbas wander while scouting into the Rock Crystal Caves. She witnessed him seizing the orb while the Elders tended a sick animal.

"I can't tell you how I acquired it," he said.

"Why give it to me? I am the one who will destroy you."

"I am the only one who knows how to use it. At least you can't destroy me without knowledge of its use," Barsabbas said, trying to convince her.

Astarta put the orb into a tin box and placed it under her bed. Barsabbas took her into his arms and kissed her passionately. She felt his barbaric strength, which pulled at her clothes and ripped the gown recently acquired by the king. Her slender body with milky white skin was exposed to him. He got up to lift her onto the bed and disrobe himself. She thought he moved gracefully; not clumsily or barbarically like his size denoted. They made love with great passion.

She felt that this could be the last loving moment they would have between them.

"Thank you, Lady Astarta. You must be careful of Barsabbas' guards," the caregiver warned her, interrupting her thoughts of Barsabbas. Caregiver Katherine took the basket from Astarta.

"Oh, you're welcome," Astarta said, but her eyes were still foggy with the memories of her warrior lover.

"There is sure a place for you in heaven, Lady Astarta," Caregiver Katherine said as she closed and locked the gate before silently walking away.

"I sure pray so," Astarta whispered as she watched the caregiver walk away.

Chapter 3
The Battle to End a King

The journey was long for Barsabbas, his entourage, and Emer. They traveled through the Hollow Knolls and past Lake Nemorosa, which was dry, dusty, and barren. It was a silent ride for all, and having Emer with him reminded Barsabbas of his evil deeds.

The first was when he had traveled through the White Mountains on a scouting mission. The king had just learned that there might be some unrest among the Drummonds and had sent him to scout out the Drummond territory. Barsabbas had a small troop of men with him, but he wandered farther than the troop. He was determined to find the Rock Crystal Caves. He had a looking glass and shone the sun light long the wall of the mountain and when the light came back he knew he had found the entrance. He had never seen such beauty in nature before. The caves looked cold, but they were warm. He realized that the illusion of the crystal was to resemble ice just as Emer had once explained to him.

He approached the center of the cave after it seemed he had traveled for hours. Then he saw the green glow. The crystals glimmered bright, and that was when he saw the Green Orb. He felt its warmth and power grow inside him. He knew that it was his for the taking. The Elders were not around. It was then that he knew he could be king.

Once the Green Orb was in his possession, the unrest with the Drummond Tribe had become more than a threat. King Viktor had traveled with his great army over the White Mountains. Barsabbas had seen the Drummond army preparing for battle. They had five adult, white-winged dragons harnessed to the ground; they blew fire into the air. The cyclops owners rode the backs of the massive creatures and controlled their every move. Hundreds of thousands of Drummonds were prepared. The trebuchets were load with lethal flaming boulders. Ballistas were cocked and ready for the call.

Barsabbas knew that this would be the battle of all battles. He looked at the beasts and knew that the Merlinians were going to have to conjure up their best magik for this battle. He remembered that Emer was not with Viktor, which made Viktor was an easy target for him, but it had to look like an accident.

The battle was fierce, and each side lost many men. The Drummonds used the dragons to create small windstorms in areas of the battle field with their wings. The trebuchets and ballistas were strategically placed so that they would hit their mark over and around the windstorms.

The Merlinians were the ones who sensed the next move and assisted in counteracting it. The Merlinians used protection spells, but the winds from the white-winged dragons were like the gales in Tricyrtis on a hot summer's day. For a time, Barsabbas could not see Viktor through the sandstorm. Then he noticed Viktor in a heated battle with the Drummond Prince Vella. He took advantage of the sandstorm and the king's heated fight with Vella to charge the king. He shoved the prince aside and battled his own king. Once he had the advantage of the fight, he sliced the head from his beloved king.

Returning to the present, Barsabbas wondered if Emer had cast a spell on him to force him to remember his deeds. He did not care either way. It was done, and he would reign as Boltonia's king with or without Emer's blessing. All his plans were falling into place.

Chapter 4

The Enlightenment

Astarta walked away from orphanage and followed the footpath out to an open field with one lone tree. She found a lone tree that the Elders had blessed with leaves. It was autumn, and the leaves had already turned vibrant colors of yellow and red. Trees had not been able to flourish in the very dry conditions. There had not been any rain for months. Water was a luxury now.

Astarta sat under the great maple tree. She wrapped herself in her cloak so that no one would notice who she was. She took out an apple that she had held aside for herself. Then, in the shade of the yellow and red leaves, she reminisced.

She had taken the Green Orb to her grandfather after the news of King Viktor's death. She knew that Barsabbas would be back for the orb. He had been correct that she did not know how to use it, but she knew her grandfather would show her how. When she showed her grandfather the orb, she saw the fear and concern in his weary eye.

"Barsabbas will be back for this. That is for certain," her grandfather told her.

Her grandfather had been the king's advisor as well as Barsabbas's, and it was believed that he was the greatest magikian and seer, like the Great Merlin. Astarta had heard Barsabbas called her grandfather Merlin in jest. Her grandfather did not take to the jokes. She knew that her grandfather was a serious Merlinian. He had been instructed by the best Merlinians in Boltonia, who had been instructed by Merlin himself.

Merlin had arrived in Boltonia and had captivated the court of King

Solmore many years before her grandfather was even a thought. Merlin had been reminded of his homeland of Briton by the landscape of Boltonia, and he made Boltonia his home for many years afterward. He instructed a gifted few, and it was believed that the Elders were the last to have seen Merlin before he had disappeared from Boltonia.

Astarta remembered her grandfather conveying tales of her birth. She had been born of the caul, and he had declared her a Benandanti. He said that he had watched Astarta as a child and knew that she had the gift to be a true Merlinian. He informed her that it was time for her to be instructed in the art of Merlin, and the training did not take long. Astarta had been using her visions effectively, and her grandfather helped her to control them.

"Astarta, magik is not what it seems. Men who cannot use their minds and use what they learned together are ignorant to our wonders and believe it to be magik. Astarta, you have to believe in yourself and your powers. It's a gift only a few are born with," her grandfather said.

Her lessons were few, because Astarta was a fast learner; the lessons came easily to her. Her grandfather told her that he believed that she was beyond a fourth-year student of Merlinian studies. Soon she had passed seventh- or eighth-year studies. It was time for her grandfather to show her the use of the Green Orb.

"The history of the Green Orb goes back to a time before the Elders. A power stronger and older than the Elders themselves forged the orb deep in the ground. No other amber has ever been found. The Elders are keepers of the Green Orb. They are the true Benandanties, Merlinians who were born of the caul. All were chosen because of the special gifts that they have. They are twelve in number. They are a force to be reckoned with. The Green Orb is the life force for all the lands of Boltonia. The abilities of the orb are far greater than you can ever imagine. Not only will it protect and cure; it can destroy as well. It was placed in the Rock Crystal Caves of the White Mountains away from us all so that no one person could use it against us," Emer instructed the attentive Astarta, though she was already aware of the history of the Green Orb.

Her grandfather took her into the hot summer's sun and demonstrated for her the powers of the Green Orb. He took the Orb in one hand and touched a dead oak tree. The tree began to glow green, and then the leaves became green with life. Her grandfather then touched the dry grass around his aged cottage, and it grew healthy again. The ivy was lifeless and limp, the leaves brittle and cracked in the sunlight, but it grew up to the thatch when touched by the old man's hand. Astarta watched in amazement.

"See, my dear? It's a powerful force that controls life in these lands. If this falls into the wrong hands, it could prove dangerous."

"Why do you think Barsabbas had it?" she asked her grandfather.

"It is a dangerous power for Barsabbas to have. You will have to go through the process of becoming a Merlinian to defeat him."

"What process?"

"One day, you will take my place as the Merlinian in this land."

"I will be the seer, magikian, and the Merlinian as Barsabbas mocks," Astarta said. She sounded disappointed by her new appointment.

"Astarta, you knew this was coming. Don't look at it as a curse. It is a great gift. Like the one Merlin himself had," her grandfather explained to her with great enthusiasm. "Merlin was a great seer but no magikian."

"Yes, yes, he was an educated man. I remembered that from your teachings when I was younger."

"Astarta, you must remember everything you were taught, and I will teach you all the rest that will make you this land's best Merlinian. Now back to the Green Orb. You saw me give life to all the dead plants around the cottage. Now, you shall learn to use the orb." Emer handed the orb to Astarta. "Take the orb in your left hand—always the left and never the right. Holding the orb in the right hand will give you fatal results. While it is cradled in your left hand, it will feel warm. It might even feel like it will burn you, but concentrate on life and touch whatever needs life."

Astarta concentrated and touched a dead sparrow that lay near the cottage. The sparrow glowed green and then life came to the small bird. It was weak at first; it stumbled to its stick-like legs. Then it flapped its wings and flew away.

"Hey, you. Beggar!" A soldier who must not have recognized Astarta interrupted her memory. Astarta stood up to answer the soldier. He was a handsome man in his early adulthood. His long reddish-blond hair flowed out of his helmet. His blue eyes squinted in the autumn sunlight. She realized that he was Liam, a young and strong warrior who was not in Barsabbas's favor, for he was human. He was to guard the villages rather than fight the great battles with his lord. This had frustrated Liam and made him a hostile soldier.

"Beggars are not to be on the paths," he said. "Get back to the village."

"Yes," Astarta said, not looking up, for fear that she would be recognized.

"Yes, what?"

"Yes, sir."

"You don't sound sure. Don't make me get down from my steed to convince you."

"No, sir. I'll be off to the village."

Astarta headed back toward the village. She didn't notice Liam following because her thoughts were on the Green Orb and her grandfather.

Chapter 5
The Hidden

Astarta knew that Barsabbas was in search of her and the orb and that he had planned to take the throne that her cousin had occupied. She also knew that Barsabbas had murdered her cousin to take the throne. She had seen all this in her visions. She had to go back to get the orb. The only reason he would want her now was for the orb. The love they had shared long before was gone, or was it? He was the first and only halfling she had ever loved. The knowledge that she would bear his child was inconceivable. How could that happen now? He no longer trusted her and hunted her like a wild animal in the Forest of Shadows. The only threat now was the orb. She had to get the orb back to the Elders.

Astarta had a vision of a great fire and her grandfather. "Grandfather," she said under her breath. In her vision, she watched Barsabbas take her grandfather and burn the cottage.

In disguise, Astarta traveled at night and alone through the Haunted Forest. This forest was the most mysterious of all forests in the lands of Boltonia and seemed unaffected by the devastation the rest of the land was enduring. It was said that it came to life after dark. Astarta had no fear of the forest, so she walked straight into it.

The trees were the tallest of all of the lands of Boltonia, and they sensed the presence of foreign entities that entered the forest and reacted to them. Special intelligence had been given to the trees by Merlin to protect his hidden residence while he had lived in Boltonia. The trees would have been more aggressive toward this intruder, but they knew it was Astarta, and that kept them at bay. The trees' bark was smooth like skin, and their branches all stretched upward, creating a canopy effect for the forest floor.

Astarta was overcome by the odors of the dampness, decomposed leaves, and enchanted flowers that invited her to come to them. All this covered the forest floor like a carpet and made each step soft.

The main flora bulk consisted of the usual varieties found in Boltonia: woodland laurel, butcher's broom, and honeysuckle.

Astarta approached the honeysuckle flowers and carefully plucked a dainty flower from the vine. She pulled the stamen away from the tubular petals and released the sweet liquid inside, letting it drop into her mouth. The enchanted liquid tingled in her mouth, and she immediately had sight in the dark.

The elder trees offered her transport within their trunks, but she graciously declined them. They did not grow together in a grove but scattered throughout the forest for weary travelers. Those who chose to use these trees for travel paid a hefty price that usually consisted of a family member or one's own life in slavery. It would not be uncommon for the trees to ask for an infant as well.

The seven white petals of the lady's nightcap flowers shone brightly in the slender beams of moonlight that shone through the canopy. Their scent attracted her. That was when she saw the Belladonna plants.

The deadly nightshade was said to be guarded by a Centaur that had been charmed. The half-man half-horse trotted around the plants. The centaur was a tall, brawny beast. His eyes looked glassy from enchantment.

Astarta thought it would be necessary, if the prophecy was to be fulfilled, to get some of their berries, because they had the power to help with childbirth. She wondered how she would get past the centaur to get the Belladonna.

She watched him trot impatiently around the Belladonna. Then he stopped to sniff the air around him. She knew that he was aware she was in the bushes. To avoid a violent introduction, she advanced toward him with her palms upward. He reared back at the sight of her.

"It's all right, my friend. I mean you no harm," she said to him with a soft, gentle voice.

"What are you doing in the forest, boy?" the Centaur asked the disguised Astarta.

"I travel to rescue my grandfather," she said. As she looked up at him, her hood slid off her head to expose her strawberry-blonde hair.

"Lady Astarta." The Centaur, though still enchanted, was aware of who she was. "You must not travel alone in these woods. It is not safe for you here."

It was apparent that the Centaur was not concerned about his duty to the Belladonna.

"Do you have a name, Centaur?" She continued to speak softly to him.

"Penlarus," he said. He came close to her to speak.

"Why are you here?" Astarta asked with concern as she reached up to touch his face.

"I am a prisoner of the elder trees," he confessed to her.

"When will they release you?"

"I have been their prisoner since I was a colt. They say nothing to me. I know nothing of my time of imprisonment."

Astarta, sadden by his tale, stroked his cheek. His eyes were closed, yet streams of tears rolled down his face. Her sadness grew to anger.

"I will return," she said.

She searched for an elder tree, and it did not take her long to find one along a pathway in the forest. She walked up to it and rubbed the smooth bark. It immediately opened a crack in its skin to allow her entry.

"I am not here for travel," she said to the willing tree. It closed the crack as quickly as it had opened it for her. "I seek answers."

There was an eerie silence, and then words appeared on the smooth bark of the tree. "What is it you seek?"

"The Centaur, Penlarus. When is he to be released from his imprisonment?"

The silence became deafening. She felt as if the elder tree would not answer her question. She stepped back from the tree.

"The Centaur is ours for eternity," the elder tree finally answered.

"Why?"

"He is payment for travel." The words appeared one by one on the bark.

"Whose travel?" Astarta waited, and the elder tree made her wait even longer than the last time. It seemed that the elder tree was thinking.

"Merlin's travel," the elder tree answered her in elfin, her native tongue.

Astarta was amazed that Merlin would use the elder trees for travel.

"Why would Merlin use the elder trees for travel?"

And yet again, Astarta waited for the answer.

"To go home." The words again appeared in Elfin.

"But this is his home."

"Briton." The name of Merlin's true home appeared on the bark. Astarta was surprised.

"That was many years ago. Please, I implore you to let the Centaur go."

"No." The answer came immediately.

"Could there be a way we could release him?" Astarta was not in the habit of begging, but she knew there had to be a way to get Penlarus released.

"A trade."

"A trade?" Astarta asked. "I have nothing to trade with you."

"Yet."

"Yet?"

"We want the child."

Astarta read the words and knew that the elder tree wanted the son who had not yet been conceived. "I cannot do that. He will be king."

The elder tree fell silent. Astarta thought the only way that they would get her son was if she delivered him to them. If she or her son never entered the forest, they would not receive the trade.

"I will agree to the trade. Now—" Before Astarta could finish her sentence, the branches of the elder tree came down and swiped at her. One of the branches left a gash in the side of her left leg. It would forever remind her of the promise she had made to the elder tree.

She set off briskly toward where she had left Penlarus. He had not moved from his post as sentry of the Belladonna plants, and she found him no longer enchanted.

"Lady Astarta, what have you done?" He asked her as she approached him.

"I have released you."

He moved to her and noticed her bleeding leg.

"What price did you pay?" Penlarus inquired with much concern.

"I promised them what they wanted," Astarta admitted.

"But he will be our king," Penlarus said to her. She looked up at him in amazement.

"How did you know what they wanted?"

"It would be the only thing the elder tree would want from you," he said to her. Then he started off along the pathway. "Travel with me, Astarta. You will be safe."

"I am going in the other direction," she confessed.

"Lady Astarta, I thank you for releasing me. I know you did it at great cost to you. When you need me, and I know you will, call for me." He handed her a horn made of bar deer antler, "You will not hear the sound, but I will. You can only use it in the Haunted Forest."

Astarta accepted the horn.

"You take your leave then?"

"I shall. I should find others of my kind. I have been away from the herd for a very long time."

"Farewell, Penlarus. Travel safe."

"Farewell to you, Lady Astarta. I will never forget." He looked at her one last time before galloping off into the thick dark forest.

Astarta continued on her quest to rescue her grandfather. As she walked the pathway for a short while, she heard footsteps behind her. She hid behind a tree and waited, but nothing—halfling or animal—walked past. This happened several more times, and she realized that the forest was playing with her. She had to play the game as well. She ignored the footsteps and kept walking. Then the footsteps became louder and faster. She kept walking at her pace. When it sounded as if the footsteps were upon her, she quickly turned around. A gust of air blew past her, stirring up dead leaves and dirt.

"You have won this round, but I don't give up that easily," she said to the forest as if it was a person. She wiped dirt from her face.

A moan came from the bushes. She approached cautiously and moved the branches to find an alrumes, a shape-shifting creature, huddled and in tears.

"Why are you crying?" she asked the tiny creature.

"It is my watch, and I cannot get you to leave the forest," the small Alrumes explained to her.

"I cannot leave. I must travel through the forest to get to my grandfather who was captured by Barsabbas," she explained.

"Barsabbas!"

"Yes, and it is very serious. I must get the Green Orb."

"You have the Green Orb?" The Alrumes stood up and wiped her face on her torn and dirty shirt. She stood no higher than the bush. Her tiny frame made her seem like a small child. Her hair was mousy brown and had leaves and other debris in it. Her face was round and full with large puffy cheeks. Her eyes were dark, almost as though her pupils and irises were the same color.

"No, I have it hidden."

"It must go back."

"I know. I will take it back."

"The Elders are very angry."

"You know the Elders?"

The Alrumes changed into a tall elder in an emerald robe. His face showed anger.

"Yes. You must take it back," the Alrumes said, as she changed back to her first form.

"I will, but I have never traveled to the Rock Crystal Caves of the White Mountains."

"I will take you there."

"You will?"

"Yes, if I cannot scare you out of the forest, I can at least keep you from coming back. Let's go boy."

"We have to get the Orb."

"We do that then we go to the White Mountains to return the Green Orb."

"So you say," Astarta whispered under her breath. She knew she had to rescue her grandfather before she took the long journey north.

When hidden by the dead of night, the Alrumes and Astarta moved through the forest. The Alrumes knew the forest and which path would be the quickest and the safest. They were quiet as they traveled.

They reached what was left of her grandfather's cottage by the dawn of the new day. The sun had not reached the cottage yet, but there was enough light to see what was left of it. The rubble was still smoldering.

Astarta's pace went from a slight jog to a run within minutes of the sight. She panted when she came to the cottage as she stared at the burnt boards and blackened field stones that had once been her grandfather's cottage. She tried to remember where her grandfather had hid the orb. She closed her eyes to bring back the memory.

"Here, my dear, help me move the bed out," Emer had said.

She had taken hold of the corner post and pulled hard. The bed had scraped the worn wooden floor. Then Emer had knelt on the dusty floorboards and loosened one to expose a small hole in the ground.

"They can burn the place down, but they can't burn the Green Orb," Astarta said to herself.

The Alrumes caught up and glanced around the devastated cottage.

"Who lived here?"

"Quiet," Astarta whispered to the Alrumes. She scrambled to where the bed had sat. A burnt cloth that once had been Emer's bedcover marked the spot. Astarta moved the rubble and lifted a loose floorboard. From beneath, the orb glowed green as if beckoning to her. Astarta took out her pouch, emptying it, and placed the Orb into it. She had to conceal it for her long journey to find her grandfather.

She was ready to make her way when she was stopped by one of the two men who had been put there to guard the cottage.

"Hey, boy, what do you have there?"

"Just some old trinkets. You know he was a magikian," Astarta said quickly, holding up her pouch.

"You shouldn't be trespassing on royal property," the soldier said.

"Royal?"

"Yes, this here is the future king's property, and that would make anything you find in there king's property. So you might as well hand it over to me."

As the soldier came closer, Astarta quickly took the orb out of the pouched, placed the orb in her right hand, and concentrated. She touched the soldier's hand as he reached out to grab her. He glowed green and then evaporated before her eyes.

The other soldier was not awake yet. She tapped him on the shoulder to wake him.

"Where did they take the old Elf who lived here?" she asked him.

Still not fully awake, the soldier said, "Back to Castle Willhaven."

"Thank you, sir. Good day."

"Hey, wait up. Who are you?" The soldier pulled at her cloak, and her strawberry-blonde hair fell around her face. "You're the old Elf's granddaughter. Barsabbas is looking for you."

"And he will continue to look," Astarta said.

She disposed of the soldier in the same manner as the first one.

"You're Emer's granddaughter," the Alrumes uttered in disbelief. She made herself take on Emer's image.

"Now you know."

"Emer is the greatest Merlinian in these lands."

"I know that. You may come with me, but you must know that I will be rescuing my grandfather."

"You must return the Green Orb first so that the lands can return to the way they were."

"Do you have a name, Alrumes?"

"Garkov."

"Garkov, this is the way we are going to do this: I am going to get my grandfather. You may come or you can go back to the forest with my sincerest gratitude."

"I must go with you to return the Green Orb. You don't know your way. You need me," Garkov said. She returned to her original form.

"Garkov, I think you will come in quite handy."

They headed toward Castle Willhaven.

Chapter 6
The Homecoming

Barsabbas, his entourage, and Emer reached their destination, Willhaven Castle, Barsabbas's birthplace. Emer remembered Barsabbas's father, Cole, who had been general of arms for King Devlin, Viktor's father. Barsabbas's father had been a giant of the Forest of Shadows. Emer also remembered Barsabbas's mother, a human, who was so beautiful. Her hair had shone in the sun, and her eyes smiled all the time. She had so badly wanted for Barsabbas to become educated, but he had had no use for books or learning. He had taken quickly to the sword instead. Emer had witnessed the young Barsabbas becoming a soldier in Viktor's army.

"I remember your parents, Barsabbas," Emer said, "your mother—beautiful for a human."

"Old Elf, your memory for the past is great, but for the now, you do not remember," Barsabbas said, with anger in his voice.

"Your grandfather was the governor of the South Lowland of Tricyrtis. He was a great man. I was just a boy—"

"Stop your rambling," Barsabbas shouted at the old Merlinian.

The drawbridge lowered to let Barsabbas and his entourage enter the large, stone castle.

Emer's body was sore from the journey. With the courtesies were over, he knew he would have to await his fate. He had seen in a vision that Astarta had already retrieved the orb and used it. She should return it to the Elders to end all the destruction. Emer realized that the foolish girl would head for Castle Willhaven to retrieve him; the prophecy would be fulfilled.

When they entered the great hall of Willhaven Castle, the fire in the wall-length fireplace was raging. Emer felt the anticipation of Astarta's arrival as he followed Barsabbas to a large table where a meager feast had already been prepared for them.

"So my old friend, sit and eat of my provisions. We will wait for Astarta's arrival," Barsabbas said confidently.

Emer watched as Barsabbas strolled over and took his seat at the head of the table. Emer slowly joined him, though not because he was hungry.

"Oh Barsabbas, you think this will be easy. It will take all the strength that you have. It will take more than your muscle to overcome this," Emer said. His words uttered came with great warning.

"You test my nerves, old Elf."

"She will test everything you have. She is not a child who will be easily persuaded to your whim."

"You forget one thing, Emer: she once loved me."

"She is stronger now than she was before. You should be worried, Barsabbas."

"She will give me an heir."

"Is that all you remember of the prophecy? She will take life from you. You will have no power to stop her."

"Emer, I will have the orb."

"How do you know you will have the orb?" Emer asked.

"Astarta will bring it to me," Barsabbas informed Emer with a smile.

Emer stared into Barsabbas's eyes and noticed the blue was not as bright as it had once been.

"You believe that my granddaughter would just hand over the orb, just like that?" Emer asked with annoyance in his voice.

"She loves me," Barsabbas said with confidence.

"Do you love her?" Emer watched the great warrior freeze.

Barsabbas took a long moment to answer his question. "I did once," Barsabbas said to convince Emer, but he saw through the lie.

"You should ask yourself if she still loves you now. You are no longer the warrior she fell in love with. Again, you should be worried about all your plans," Emer warned. He could see that it struck home deep within Barsabbas.

Then the warrior and the halfling Elf sat silently at the table.

Chapter 7
The Arrival

Astarta arrived at Castle Willhaven with Garkov by her side. The ancient castle sat alone amid a vast wasteland. With the rising sun, it looked more sinister and frozen than it did in the dark. The two figures were miniscule next to the enormous building.

"Lady Astarta, I don't want to go in," Garkov said to her with the voice of a child.

Astarta thought for a moment before saying, "You really have no use for me in there. I will only need you after I rescue my grandfather." Then she proceeded toward the castle, but Garkov was stopped.

"Are you forgetting something, Lady Astarta?" Garkov asked her with the voice of an elderly man. Astarta realized she still had the Green Orb.

"I don't think I should take this with me," she said. She turned, took the pouch out from under her cloak, and handed it to Garkov. "Take care of yourself, my alrumes. Stay hidden until I return for you."

Garkov headed to boulders and hid while Astarta looked up at the enormous dark castle. They moved carefully so that the guards did not see them.

She proceeded toward the drawbridge. She found the drawbridge closed, so she had to find another way into the castle without being noticed. She sat silently, hidden behind one of the large pillars that marked the entrance to the castle. She heard the guards change, and then it fell silent again. The clang of the chains of the drawbridge alerted her that the drawbridge was to be lowered. As it reached the ground before her, she looked for any traffic for the bridge. There was no movement inside or outside the castle.

It would seem that either Emer was helping her or Barsabbas knew she had arrived. She cautiously crossed the drawbridge and entered the castle within the shadows. Her movements were smooth and quick.

She stopped to glance into the great hall. She saw both men seated at the table. She could not contain her excitement of seeing her grandfather safe and well. She entered the hall and ran to her grandfather. She gave him a kiss of affection and held onto him tightly.

"Thank you for joining us, Astarta," Barsabbas said.

"I am here to rescue my grandfather—"

Before she could finish her sentence, Barsabbas interrupted her, "Rescue? Your grandfather is not a prisoner; he is my guest."

Astarta gave her grandfather a puzzled look.

"A guest?"

"Astarta, you do remember a promise you made to me?" Barsabbas asked her. "You're not going to break that promise, are you?"

"Barsabbas wants to have the wedding," Emer said. Astarta noticed that he could not look her in the eyes.

"How can I marry him, Grandfather? He is not the Barsabbas I once loved. Beside, Viktor was to marry us."

"Emer has agreed to take over the ceremony," Barsabbas said.

"Grandfather, you didn't?"

Emer took Astarta's two hands into his and looked into her eyes.

"It is time, my dear," he said.

Astarta felt herself going into a trance. She was taken far from the great hall to a land of beauty. Bright white lights flew around her head. She realized that Emer was passing his power to her. She began to see a vision, a message from Emer of a plan to escape.

"Pull them apart, quickly," Barsabbas commanded.

The guards pulled the grandfather from his granddaughter.

"Emer, don't do that again until I command you to do so. Now, both of you get prepared for the wedding."

Astarta was dazed and weak from the failed attempt. She could not move for a few moments.

"My lord, I have a wedding present for you," a voice came from outside the great hall. Liam walked into the great hall with the Alrumes, Garkov.

"No, Garkov," Astarta whispered under her breath.

"You brought me an Alrumes?" Barsabbas was disgusted at the sight of the small creature.

"No, my lord, it is what is in her possession that I think you would appreciate," Liam announced as he held up the small Alrumes by the collar of her torn and dirty shirt.

"Give it to our king," Liam commanded.

"He's no king of mine," Garkov said.

As Liam was about to strike the small creature, Astarta felt her grandfather stop Liam with his mind.

"My friend of the forest, would you do this Merlinian a favor and give me the Green Orb?" Emer said gently to the small Alrumes.

"Oh, great Emer, this orb belongs to the Elders," Garkov said innocently.

"I know it does, but to save your life, I need to take it from you."

Astarta watched as Emer walked up to the small creature to take the orb from the trusting Garkov. She watched in horror as Garkov handed him the pouch with the orb in it.

"Give it to me, Emer," Barsabbas commanded.

"Against my better judgment, I will surrender it to you," Emer said, reluctantly handing the orb to Barsabbas. Liam threw the Alrumes to the ground. Astarta ran to Garkov.

"Lady Astarta, why did great Emer give what is the Elders to Barsabbas?

"My grandfather has a plan," she whispered into Garkov's ear. The small Alrumes listened to the plan whispered in her ear.

"I understand, Lady Astarta, I will do as you say," Garkov said.

Chapter 8
The Hieros Gamos

They all left the great hall to their designated dressing chambers. Astarta stared at the wedding gown that Barsabbas had selected for her to wear. The gown had been handsewn by the seamstresses of Verbena from the finest silk. It was pure white with an emerald-green silk sash. An emerald-encrusted tiara sat upon the table and shimmered in the firelight. Her veil had been a gift from her mother, given to her the night that Barsabbas had asked for her hand. It had been the one her mother wore on her wedding day. The wedding was all she used to hope for, but now it was like a terrible dream that she could not wake up from. She prayed to the Elders that they would give her the strength to go through with the wedding and her grandfather's plan.

Barsabbas was in the great hall directing his servants, enslaved Elves, to prepare the hall for the wedding. The windows to the great hall were opened to let in a soft breeze. Opposite the windows was the fireplace, where a raging fire blazed. A large barrel of rainwater sat at one end of the room, and opposite that across the hall sat a wagon full of soil from the home of Astarta's birth. Barsabbas used the Green Orb to bring life to dead flowers that his servants had picked from the once vibrant gardens of Willhaven Castle. Green satin ribbons adorned the aisle that Astarta would walk down to the center of the hall. Benches and chairs of dried amber wood formed a circle around the center of the great hall. Servants were in the kitchen preparing food that Barsabbas had enchanted from the vegetable garden and the barn.

He was now able to give life and take it away with a touch of his hand. He was content at that moment. He had the stolen prize that would give him the power he needed to conquer the lands and the woman who had stolen his heart. He sat upon one of the dried chairs, and it creaked as though in pain while it held the weight of this huge halfling. He looked around the room, proud of what he had accomplished. He thought how easy it had all come to him, without fighting and with little effort.

Emer was in his chambers looking over his attire for the wedding. It was the Merlinian robe that he had worn in Viktor's court. The emerald green had shown bright within his family's tartan. The robes had been designed so that every Merlinian would have a piece of Merlin and his own family with him. As he lowered his eyes to the floor, he caught a glimpse of a flowing emerald robe passing. He looked up to see Merlin standing before him.

"Merlin, is that you?" the old Elf asked the figure.

The figure towered over Emer.

"Do not forget your plan, my son."

"It appears to me that an Alrumes is playing tricks on me," Emer said as Garkov returned to her own shape and looked up at Emer.

"Oh, great Emer, you need not worry. Your plan will save Lady Astarta and all of these lands."

"From your mouth to the Elders' ears, my small Alrumes."

"We will do it for the Elders. They are very unhappy that the Green Orb has been stolen."

"I know that, small one. Yet I don't know if I have the strength to fight anymore."

The Alrumes took the form of King Viktor.

"You need to be strong, Grandfather," he said, "for my kingdom is in peril. You and Astarta must fight for me."

"You are very good, Garkov. That is what my grandson would have said to me."

Garkov returned to her form, looking like a child.

"Great Emer, do not give up hope. You know what our lands will be like if Barsabbas becomes king and the Green Orb is not returned."

"Yes, I do," Emer said to the Alrumes. He stood and steadied himself to put on his Merlinian robe for the wedding.

The time had come for Astarta to take the walk she had waited so long to take. She wore her lavish wedding gown. Her strawberry-blonde hair could be seen through her mother's veil, and upon her head sat the emerald tiara. As she turned the corner and looked down the aisle, she could see Barsabbas outfitted in his general of arms uniform and her grandfather in his Merlinian robe.

She walked down the aisle to the sound of music. She did not look at anyone in the hall except for Barsabbas. He was still handsome in his uniform. She remembered the good times they had had together and how he had loved her. Then she stood before the man she had once loved and her wise grandfather, ready to be married. It was not how she had pictured this day.

"Before us stands Barsabbas, general of arms, and Lady Astarta of the royal court of King Viktor," Emer announced. Astarta saw Barsabbas glare at Emer, but her grandfather ignored the glare and continued. "They will come together on this day to become halfling and wife. May the Elders look upon this union and give them their blessings," Emer said.

Then he stopped and looked at Barsabbas.

"My love, Astarta, you are the power within me. I live, breathe, and fight for you. I will love, honor, respect, and protect you and my future heirs. You will be in my life now and for always. I love you."

The guests applauded Barsabbas.

Emer looked over at Astarta and gave her a wink. She was not prepared to say anything or to profess a love that no longer existed.

She looked up and into Barsabbas's eyes. She noticed that they were not bright blue but a dark gray. She moved from Barsabbas and looked out toward the guests. She started to speak.

"Thank you all for being part of our special day. This is the day that Barsabbas and I have been waiting for. It was supposed to be my cousin, King Viktor, who presided over the ceremony, but my kind and wise grandfather has graciously stepped in." She moved over to Barsabbas and took his large hands before continuing, "You are the only halfling I have ever loved." She looked deep into his eyes as she had when she had been in love with him. "May we be together and be in this much love until the end of our days. I promise to love, honor, respect, and protect you and our heirs."

Emer took the ceremonial wedding rope and tied their hands together.

"With this ceremonial rope, your lives are forever tied together. You will be one in all that you do. All that is his is yours. All that is hers is yours."

Emer finished the ceremony, and Barsabbas and Astarta kissed. The guests applauded once more.

When the evening's festivities came to a close, Barsabbas led Astarta to the bedchamber. They had not spoken since the ceremony nor had been alone together until then.

"You know that this had to happen," Barsabbas said.

"Why, Barsabbas? Why have you done all this to me, to Viktor, to my grandfather, and to our people?"

"You won't understand," he said. His back was toward her.

"Oh, you don't think so; I know you. I have seen inside you. You are not the Barsabbas general of arms, which I fell so deeply in love with. You are different. We could have been happy. But you weren't happy enough just to love me. You had to have power to go along with it. You had to have the Green Orb."

"You make me very happy, but I wanted to rule over and command all the lands, and I can be a great king. With you at my side, we will be great," he said to her. Then he turned around and went to her.

"You were great to me but not anymore."

Barsabbas knelt before Astarta and looked up into her eyes.

"Can you ever love me again?" he asked.

"You need to ask yourself how you can change enough for me to love you again. If you cannot become the Barsabbas I once loved, then this arrangement is as dry and dead as the lands around us. I would prefer my own bedchamber."

Barsabbas reluctantly granted Astarta her own bedchamber.

Chapter 9
The Plan

Astarta entered her bedchamber alone. She was there only a moment before she heard a knock at the chamber door.

"Lady Astarta, please let me in," came the familiar voice of Garkov.

She opened the door to find one of Barsabbas's guards standing before her.

"It is I, Lady Astarta," Garkov said as she returned to her child-like form and entered the room.

"Garkov, you must summon my grandfather to my chamber. Please be careful, Garkov," she said.

Then Garkov took the form of a guard once again.

"I will, Lady Astarta."

Garkov left the chamber. It seemed like an eternity before Astarta heard a knock on the chamber door.

"Who's there?" Astarta asked through the door.

"It is Garkov, Lady Astarta."

She opened the door to reveal Garkov and her grandfather, and they quickly entered the chamber.

"Astarta, we need to do this before anyone notices," her grandfather said. She took her grandfather's hands as they had done in the great hall when she first arrived. "My dear, it is time for you to become a Merlinian." Emer looked into his granddaughter's eyes.

Astarta was once again transported to a beautiful land of growing wild flowers with a sweet aroma. Trees were full of fruit ready to be picked. The valley below was rich with golden grain. She turned around to see an elderly man in an emerald robe in the distance. He wore a pointed hat upon his head. She approached him.

"Merlin?" she asked.

"Yes, it is I," he said. "You are to receive all of your grandfather's wisdom and power."

"What will happen to him?"

"He will no longer be Emer the Great."

"He will still be Emer, my grandfather?"

"My child, once the power is given, there will be nothing left of him," he said. Merlin spoke from experience.

"No, I need him."

"This is now your battle to win," Merlin said. Then he left her just as he had appeared to her. She was alone. She felt warm, and her skin tingled. She closed her eyes to cry, and when she opened them she was back in her chamber. She was so afraid to let her grandfather's hands go. She could feel his weight fall back, and she eased her grandfather to the floor.

His eyes opened, and he looked at her.

"Astarta, listen to me. You must fulfill the prophecy. You must give Barsabbas an heir. The great rite must take place."

"But, Grandfather, I can't."

"You must. Your heir will be where my soul will go. I must leave you, but I will be a lost if the heir is not born of your union with Barsabbas."

"I don't understand."

"A Merlinian may transfer power, but the soul must be transferred by birth. Astarta, you must do this. Then you must go to the Elders, they will help you with the rest of the plan."

Through her tears, she agreed to do as her grandfather requested.

"Don't leave me," she cried out.

"I must. You have my powers. You are now stronger and wiser. I must go and wait for the day I return as your son. Go. Do what I have asked you to do."

Astarta stood before her grandfather and watched him fade away. Nothing was left in the place where he had lain. She cried until she felt a tug on her gown by Garkov.

"Lady Astarta, it is time," Garkov said.

"Yes, Garkov, it is."

Astarta left the bedchamber that she had requested and went to the bedchamber she was to share with Barsabbas.

He was already in the bed and sleeping. In the dark, she disrobed and got into bed. She awoke Barsabbas with a kiss of affection.

"You came back to me," he whispered.

"I will always come back to you, Barsabbas. You are the halfling I will always love."

Chapter 10
The Escape

The sun shone into the bedchamber to find Astarta alone in her wedding bed. Barsabbas had risen early and left without a word. It was how he usually left her. Why would he change his behavior? She put both of her hands on her abdomen and felt the life inside her. It had happened. She was with child, a male. A smile came to her face, whether from joy that she knew she was having a child or that she had the power she received from her grandfather to know the child was there, or even both. She called for Garkov with her mind and heard a small knock at the door.

"Garkov, is that you?" Astarta asked through the door.

"Yes, Lady Astarta. I heard you call me."

Astarta let Garkov into the bedchamber. She looked like a guard again but returned to her form once in the room.

"It is done," Astarta said.

The Alrumes touched Astarta's abdomen.

"The child is there."

"Yes, Garkov. You know what you need to do."

"Yes, Lady Astarta." Garkov did not hesitate to take on Lady Astarta's appearance.

"Remember, Garkov, you must grow with me or Barsabbas will know that you are not me. I will let you know when to grow."

"What if Barsabbas realizes I am not you?"

"He won't. He has no sight. He cannot see into you like I can. You are

36

very loyal, my Alrumes. Do as I do, grow as I grow, and you will not be found out. I must leave you now before I will not be able to leave."

"Do be careful, Lady Astarta. You hold inside you our salvation."

"I know that."

It was early morning and Astarta knew that Barsabbas and his soldiers would be out training in the dry empty field on the south side of the castle. The guards would not question her if she moved through the castle now that she was Barsabbas's wife. Once she reached the drawbridge she carefully checked the guard that was positioned on the allure. As the guard turned his back she disguised herself as the boy and ran. She headed north toward the White Mountains.

She felt a presence following her, so she moved carefully along the road. When the presence became stronger, she stopped and hid for a while to wait. She caught a glimpse of Liam following her on foot. She went to him.

"What are you doing out here, Liam?" Astarta asked him sternly.

"I might ask the same of you, Lady Astarta," his answer came swift, quick and as stern as her question to him.

"You must go back and say nothing about having seen me."

She turned her back on him and continued her journey, but he continued to follow.

"What are you doing following me?" Astarta stopped and turned to him.

"I am here to protect you," Liam said with concern.

"Why would you do that?"

"You carry our king."

"How do you know that?" She was surprised.

"The Merlinians are not the only ones who know of the prophecy," he said.

"I do not need any protection. I am a Merlinian now," she said. She turned and walked on.

"You will need help in the White Mountains."

"Even giving Barsabbas the orb did not get you what you wanted?"

"How did you know?"

"I am a Merlinian."

"Can I ask you a question?"

"You just did."

Liam shook his head.

"What did you see in that barbarian?"

"That barbarian you called 'my lord'?"

"You didn't answer my question."

"He was different when Viktor was alive. He was a strong warrior, but he was so gentle with me. He loved me."

"Doesn't he now?"

"All he loves is power and that orb. And you gave it to him. You could have taken it back to the Elders and saved us all and become a hero."

"Then the prophecy would not be fulfilled, and we would still have no king."

"A king."

"I also wanted Barsabbas's respect," Liam continued his confession.

"You will never get that. Not now."

"What will you do once you reach the Elders?"

"Fulfill the prophecy. I was told by my grandfather to seek help from the Elders."

"Where is the great Emer?" he asked her. She stopped walking. She looked down at the ground and did not answer. Then she continued to walk.

Liam did not question her anymore; he just followed.

It was dark before they reached the base of the White Mountains. They still had to climb up to locate the Rock Crystal Caves. She felt good and she wanted to climb, but it was too dark, so they stopped for the night. In the morning, there was no sun after their rest. The clouds were all around them.

Liam started a fire and prepared some wild pheasant that he hunted for them to eat.

"What are you doing?" she asked Liam as he prepared the food.

"We cannot climb the mountain now," he said. "And we sure cannot climb it with empty stomachs."

"We do not have time for that," she said angrily.

"You are with child. You need to eat."

Liam was showing Astarta a caring side of himself that she had not seen before. She realized that he was right: she must take care of herself and her child. She sat down near the fire and watched Liam prepare the pheasant. They ate together in silence.

When the skies cleared, it was another day without rain and without water.

They started their ascent along the pathway that winded up the mountain side. They passed tall trees that were devoid of any life.

"Look at all of this," Astarta said, her voice quivering as she pointed the trees out to Liam. He stopped to look.

"This is all Barsabbas's fault. He did this by stealing the Green Orb."

Astarta watched Liam scan the landscape. Though they were not above the tree line, they could see much of Boltonia so barren and vast. There was no shimmer of blue anywhere and no green grass or golden field of grain. Astarta realized that Boltonia was dying. It was a sight that she had never thought she would see.

Astarta and Liam looked over Boltonia with much despair. They looked at each other. Astarta's tears were the only liquid that had touched the ground of Boltonia since the Green Orb had been stolen. Liam moved to Astarta's side and embraced her. He took her face in his hands and looked at it. He gently wiped the tears way with his thumbs.

They continued their journey with more determination than before. They needed to find the Rock Crystal Caves to get the Elders' help. They ascended the pathway further, and when they reached the tree line, all of Boltonia was visible. More land could be seen. Buildings speckled the landscape with no sign of life. It looked cold and lonely.

The Rock Crystal Caves were hidden, and only a true Merlinian could find them, or so Astarta thought. Astarta concentrated on the caves. They still were not in the right place. They moved farther along the path. Astarta moved her hand along the wall of the mountainside, feeling for the warmth that was said to be in the Rock Crystal Caves. The wall was cold. *Of course, it is cold,* she thought. *The Green Orb is gone.* It was what made the Rock Crystal Caves warm.

The sun was overhead and beating down on them, but Astarta could not locate the entrance. Liam watched as she frantically searched.

"It should be here. I can feel it."

"Crystals shimmer in the sunlight?" Liam asked her.

"Yes, they do," she said as she continued to search. She did not notice Liam retrieve a looking glass from his satchel and begin reflecting sunlight onto the side of the mountain until a bright light came back to him.

"I found the entrance," Liam announced to Astarta.

"How did you …?" she started to say before she looked over and saw Liam waving the looking glass back and forth on the cliff. "Only a Merlinian can find the Rock Crystal Caves."

"A Merlinian may be able to find the Rock Crystal Caves if the Green Orb is in there, but a resourceful soldier can find crystals. Now you have to find the Elders."

They entered the Rock Crystal Caves and wandered the caverns for quite a while. The crystal sparkled even without light. They stayed in the center of the pathways and cautiously stayed away from the jagged crystals that protruded from the walls. The pathways led them deep into the mountain until they reached the center, where the Green Orb had been. Only an empty pedestal remained. It was an enormous circular room with a hole at the top where the sunlight shone through. The crystals shimmered and sparkled in the sun's light. Astarta and Liam looked upward and saw the blue of the sky.

"Okay, Merlinian, where are the Elders?" Liam asked with concern.

"They are near. I feel them."

Astarta moved to a pathway off to the right and entered another circular room with twelve large chairs made of the mountain's crystals carved into the walls of the cave. All of the chairs were empty excepted for one.

"So, Astarta, you have found us," the lone Elder greeted her. He was a tall, slender man with graying hair and beard. His robe was emerald green with the crest of his family.

"Where are the others?" she asked the Elder.

"I am the one they sent to welcome you. I am Nebo. I will be taking you to the Drummonds."

"What? They are our enemy," Liam said. He was reluctant to go with the Elder.

"Why are they your enemy?" the Elder asked.

"They attacked the kingdom," Liam said.

"I believe you have been misled," the elder said before explaining, "the Drummonds are the Elders' protectors."

"Then why did King Viktor go into battle against them?" Astarta asked.

"Viktor was under the impression that the Drummonds were hostile, that they did not want the Alliance to continue. The Alliance wanted to become the protectors of the Elders. You have to understand, the Drummonds were the first people of Boltonia. They were here when the Green Orb was created. It was the Drummonds who appointed the Elders."

"Who would want to change the protectors of the Elders?" Liam asked.

"I know. Barsabbas," Astarta said.

"And the Drummonds are preparing to take back the Green Orb," Nebo added.

"Is that really necessary?" Astarta asked. "Isn't it I who will bring the end to Barsabbas?"

"You cannot do it without an army. The Drummonds are your army," Nebo said.

They left the Rock Crystal Caves and traveled over to the other side of the mountain. When they reached the edge of the Drummond hamlet of Gardinia the sun was deep in the west. The three entered the hamlet and went to the main curia. They were surrounded by the inhabitants. The Drummonds were a common people of very few luxuries. Not a word was spoken. In unison, the large group fell to one knee to salute.

"They are bowing to their new king," Nebo informed Astarta.

"How do they know?" Liam asked Astarta.

"As you informed me previously, the Merlinians are not the only ones who know about the prophecy," Astarta said.

The Drummond Prince Vella approached them. He was a prime example of a true Drummond—Halfling Dwarves covered in matted hair that looked dirty. His body was full of muscles that protruded through his clothing. A true Dwarf was short and ugly, but the Drummonds were not full Dwarves. Most of the Drummonds were halflings. They had, over the years, bred with humans and a few with Elves. Prince Vella was halfling Dwarf and Elf. He was taller than most of the Drummonds. His skin was pale white. He was confident, strong, and wise for his years.

"Lady Astarta, we welcome you to our humble hamlet. We will protect you and teach you our ways," he announced to her as he looked deep into her eyes of green. Astarta examined his face, which was long. She looked deep into his black eyes and felt the sincerity in his statement.

"Prince Vella, my escort, Liam of Verbena."

Prince Vella looked Liam over.

"Soldier of Barsabbas and a human … you will have to prove yourself to me."

"I am Lady Astarta's protector," Liam said.

"Not anymore. She is among the Drummonds. We will be her protectors. You are welcome to study our way of war and one day be worthy of the Drummonds."

Liam looked ready to hit him, but Astarta stopped him with the power of her mind. She needed Liam as well as the Drummonds. They were all working toward a common cause: to get the Green Orb back to the Elders, where it belonged.

Chapter 11

The Disguised

In the form of Astarta, Garkov took her seat next to Barsabbas in the great hall as Barsabbas was given information from a scout of his armies that the Drummonds had reinforced their armies.

"What are they up to?" Barsabbas whispered under his breath.

"The spy inside the Drummond village has reported that the king of Boltonia has arrived," the scout continued.

"They must be mad. I am the king of Boltonia," Barsabbas declared.

Garkov sat silent, watching fearfully.

"Get me, Emer," Barsabbas commanded.

"Yes, my lord."

"My love, the only one who can see into that village is your grandfather," Barsabbas said. He leaned in for a kiss, which Garkov gave him willingly.

It seemed like a lengthy amount of time before the scout came back to inform Barsabbas that Emer could not be found.

"Astarta, do you know where your grandfather has gone?"

Garkov did not know how to answer the question. She felt something take over. She knew it was Astarta. She had used her power to speak through Garkov's body.

"I am not my grandfather's keeper. You know that my grandfather is a great Merlinian. He will not stay if he does not want to stay."

"Find him," Barsabbas commanded the scout, who scrambled to leave the hall.

"Barsabbas, what should we call our son?" Astarta said through Garkov to change the subject at hand.

"He should have a strong name, a name of nobility."

"I was thinking Auberon."

"I will have to think on that. I know that the prophecy is partly fulfilled."

"Oh, Barsabbas, I am with you now. I feel so much love, I cannot think of some silly prophecy."

"You never thought it was a silly prophecy."

"You must not worry about what I thought. It is what I think now. I am tired; I will retire to the bedchamber. I must keep up my strength." Garkov got up to exit the great hall. She turned to Barsabbas and smiled. In her head, she thanked Astarta for her help.

At the Drummond village, Astarta started to fall. Liam caught her before she hit the ground. Astarta felt his muscular arms and looked up into his blue eyes. He lifted her upright again while the two held a loving glance.

Chapter 12
The Drummonds

Gardinia was not an ordinary hamlet. The dwellings were holes carved out of the mountainside. The Drummonds were blacksmiths, and they mined and forged their own tools and utensils as well as all their armor and weaponry. They mined their metals from the caverns of their homes. It was continuous labor for the Drummonds. It was what they had known all their lives. The males and females worked equally and fought equally.

Prince Vella took Liam and a large group of Drummonds to an open field that was on the other side of the White Mountains. Large artillery was being moved by another large group of Drummonds. The Drummond armies were practicing battle routines so they would be prepared.

"Liam, do you see how we prepare for battle?" Prince Vella scanned the field.

"It is impressive," Liam said.

"This is not how we spend our days. It is only after the Green Orb was stolen that we had to prepare. We are peaceful people. Only a group of us, specially chosen, would be training for a situation that would cause us to defend the Green Orb. If only I had ended Barsabbas's life, my people could go back to living peaceful lives."

Prince Vella commanded the group that followed them to take their positions on the field. Liam watched how each and every male and female worked together to become a menacing force. It was nothing Liam had ever seen before. Where Liam came from, the females were left behind during war to care for children and tend to matters of the home.

Prince Vella looked up toward the White Mountains and hollered the Drummond battle cry. Out from the cliffs flew five white-winged dragons ridden by the Cyclops. They landed in front of the prince and his companion.

"These are our best weapons."

"Dragons?"

"Yes, dragons. These may be the only dragons left in Boltonia," Prince Vella said. Then he patted one of the white-winged dragons on its nose.

"They are beautiful."

"Oh, do not mistake their beauty. They are fierce flying warriors."

While Liam was with Prince Vella touring the armies, Astarta was with the Drummonds in the hamlet. She entered the dwelling of some of the Drummonds. The dwelling was simple with only necessities that kept the Drummond way of life comfortable. There was one long banquet table, for they all ate together. Food was prepared by both males and females. All chores were shared among the inhabitants. The females mined and forged the metals. Astarta watched the metals being melted and forged into swords, axes, and giant arrowheads for the arrows for ballistas. They also weaved cloth and tailored their own clothing, though not from the silks and satins that Astarta was used to. They used materials from the pounded bark of trees and reeds from the riverbeds. These materials were becoming scarce now that the Green Orb was not in its rightful place.

Their high priestess, Zarya, came to meet with Astarta. She was a Merlinian Dwarf, and she was smaller than Astarta. Her eyes were black, and she was covered with soft, smooth white hair.

"Welcome, Lady Astarta. I am High Priestess—"

"Zarya," Astarta interjected.

"You must pardon me; I have to get accustomed to you now being a Merlinian." Zarya bowed before Astarta.

"You must not worry about that. We need to plan for what lies ahead."

"Barsabbas will not take to losing."

"He knows he is going to lose, but he doesn't know when."

Chapter 13

The King Has Come

The weather in the White Mountains was brutal, and the winter was worse. Even the lack of snow did not make survival easy. The winds were forceful and hostile. This weather had made the Drummonds firm and strong warriors.

Liam observed and practiced with the Drummonds, and became a mighty warrior as well. He became educated in all the weaponry of the Drummonds. His favorite was the scimitar. He would spar for hours with Prince Vella until the prince thought him worthy.

Astarta practiced with both of them until her body could not bear the exertion. The king inside her had to be protected and grow. Then she was sent to study with Zarya until it was time for her to pick up the sword once more.

When the days grew brighter and longer, preparations for the Ostara celebration started. The Drummonds who were not involved in training for the battle were occupied with duties preparing for the holiday. The feast was small, for it contained only what was left after the long winter.

After the feast, Astarta and Liam went for a walk along one of the many caverns in the home of their host. Liam spent his days with the Drummond warriors, but he spent his evenings with Astarta. Liam's interest in Astarta had grown into a longing for her. He hoped that Astarta viewed him in a different light now. He had been an angry young man, but during his stay with the Drummonds, his anger had shifted. The anger had been directed toward Barsabbas, where it should have been all along. He wondered if Astarta could be interested in a simple human.

"You grow more beautiful every day," Liam said to her as he laid his hand on her enlarged abdomen. Liam was the only one she allowed to touch her unborn child.

"Liam, I grow so large. I feel that I will burst, yet you find me beautiful," Astarta said. Liam caught her blushing. He gently stroked her strawberry-blonde hair and caressed her cheeks with his hands.

"Astarta, you know why I followed you from the village that day?"

"You knew it was me?" she asked.

"You could not fool me with that disguise. You still walked like a woman."

"Well, one day, you must teach me how to walk like a man," she said. They both giggled.

"I watched you once, in the market. You had stolen some bread from that huge baker. You did like to test him. Then I saw you take your hood off and let out your hair," Liam spoke to her with a gentle voice. He took her locks in his hand and brought her hair to his nose to smell. The sweet smell of lilac filled his senses. "I was, well … in love."

Liam stared into her eyes, which sparkled blue at that moment. He moved in to kiss her, and she let him. He embraced her as tightly as he could because of her size. He wished that the moment would never end, but he knew they had to get back to the celebration.

The dancing and celebration went into the night. Not one Drummond seemed tired from their labors. It was time to give thanks for the rebirth of their lands, as they did every spring. They were mindful that this spring might not be the spring they were used to though.

Astarta and Liam were enjoying the festivities when it happened. Astarta grabbed her large abdomen. The sharp pain she felt made her cry out.

"What is it, Astarta?" Liam asked.

"The child wants to be born."

"The child?"

Zarya ran to Astarta's side.

"We must get her to my home for the birth."

They moved quickly to Zarya's home and made Astarta comfortable.

"Now, you must go," Zarya told Liam.

"I will not leave her."

"Listen to me. This will not be a pretty thing for you to see. I have had warriors hardier than you get sick on me. I do not have time to take care of her, the king, and you. Now go."

Liam moved to outside the door and posted himself as guard.

It was not until the sun shone and the sky was pink that a child's cry could be heard within the dwelling. Zarya came out to him.

"The king is here. Give word to Prince Vella," Zarya commanded Liam, who moved to find the prince.

When Liam was able to locate him, he told the prince, "The king is here."

"The battle will be soon," Prince Vella said. The he entered the main curia, and a crowd of Drummonds grouped around him. "The king has come, and the battle will be soon," the prince said.

The Drummond crowd cheered.

"We must prepare," Prince Vella said to Liam as he followed the prince out of the curia.

"I must see Astarta," Liam said.

The prince stopped.

"Do what you must," he said. "Do you love her?"

"Yes."

"Good," the prince said, "because if you didn't …"

The prince continued away without finishing his statement.

Zarya was attending to child and mother when Liam entered her dwelling.

"How are they doing?" Liam whispered to Zarya.

"They are both resilient," Zarya whispered back. "You can see them."

Liam knelt at Astarta's bedside and gazed at her and the new king.

"What is his name?" Liam asked her in a whisper.

"Auberon," she said.

Chapter 14

The Disappearance

Garkov received a message from Astarta that the king had been born. It was time to escape from Willhaven Castle as soon as she could. This was not an impossible task for the little Alrumes, who could disguise herself as a guard and walk out of the castle. It had to be planned though. She could not just stop what she was doing. That would bring attention to her. She had to make it so that Barsabbas wouldn't search for her, Astarta, or the king.

On the day of the Grand Council of all governors, councilors, and Merlinians of Boltonia, no one was to enter the council chamber while Barsabbas addressed them. They were planning his coronation.

"We will have the coronation after the birth of my heir," Barsabbas informed his council.

"When is the child due?" a councilman asked.

"Any day now so preparations should be made."

"Have you obtained Viktor's crown?" another member of the council inquired.

"The Crown of Boltonia has been in my possession since Viktor's demise," Barsabbas said to the council with an evil grin. His eyes were completely gray.

"And what of the orb?" Randolf the Merlinian asked. "We will need it to defeat the Drummonds." Randolf was a Merlinian, in ill favor with the other Merlinians of Boltonia, employed by Barsabbas.

"I possess that as well," Barsabbas said confidently. "We will have no problem with the Drummonds."

"The scouts have witnessed great movement among the Drummonds," the governor of Verbena said.

"Yes, I am curious as to what they are up to," Barsabbas said. "Randolf, what do you see?"

Randolf went into a vision and witnessed the battle with the Drummonds. *It was hot and sandstorms were whipping his eyes. He saw a boy with a scimitar, and he wielded it with great ease. A battle with Barsabbas and the boy ensued. The sand blinded Randolf then.* The vision was gone.

"My lord, you will battle a boy," Randolf informed Barsabbas.

"With all their warriors, the Drummonds send a boy?" Barsabbas laughed, and it echoed in the great council chamber. "This will be easy and quick."

Garkov waited outside the great council chamber for the governors, council members, and the Merlinians to leave. Barsabbas was still in counsel with Randolf once they were gone.

"Have you found Emer?" Barsabbas asked Randolf with great concern.

"My lord, the process was completed, and Emer is no more," Randolf said.

"When did this occur?"

"My lord, I cannot tell."

"I think I know. Summon Astarta."

As Randolf exited the great council chamber, Garkov transformed into a guard. It was time. She had to leave before Barsabbas realized what had transpired.

She escaped the castle and headed into the White Mountains, but not before letting Astarta know what had just taken place in the castle.

Chapter 15

The Betrayal

It was not long before Randolf frantically returned to the great council chamber.

"My lord, she is gone."

"What do you mean she is gone?" Barsabbas stood up and looked down at Randolf. "Find her," he commanded him.

Randolf went into a vision. *He saw the Drummonds celebrating and then preparing for battle. He could not see Garkov, Astarta, or the child in his vision. He did see Liam preparing for battle with the Drummonds.*

"I see a traitor, Liam the human. He is preparing for battle with the Drummonds," Randolf revealed to Barsabbas.

"Where is Astarta?" Barsabbas shouted at Randolf.

"I don't see her. If the process has taken place, she is more powerful than I am and will shield herself and anyone she pleases. But if my visions are taking me to the Drummonds, she must be there."

"Take leave of me."

"My lord, what about the traitor?" Randolf asked Barsabbas.

"I will take care of the traitor on the battlefield. We must prepare for battle. Call my general of arms."

Randolf once again left the great council chamber.

Barsabbas sat alone in anger because of the betrayal by the woman he had loved. Hatred grew inside him for her and for Liam. It consumed him. His hair, once raven black, turned a grayish white. He decided that Astarta and Liam would die with the Drummonds.

Randolf reentered the chamber with the general of arms. They both noticed the change in Barsabbas's hair color but said nothing.

"What do we face?" Barsabbas asked Barrett, his general of arms. Barrett, a halfling from a human and a giant from the Dark Forest, stood as tall as Barsabbas. He also had the blue eyes and raven black hair that Barsabbas had once possessed.

"The Drummonds have the dragons that we are not able to defeat," Barrett informed Barsabbas.

"I will be able to defeat them. You must make it possible for me to reach them."

"With the Merlinians we possess, they should make that possible, my lord."

"Randolf will be with me at all times. I will have the Green Orb."

"You will bring it into battle, my lord?" Barrett asked.

"It will be what we need to take down those dragons and the Drummonds once and forever. Just make sure there is a path for me to get to them."

"With the winds they produce, it will be a challenge."

"A challenge you will overcome, Barrett. Enough talk. We must prepare. The Drummonds are waiting for us."

Chapter 16

It All Comes to This

Not long after the birth of her son, the king of Boltonia, Astarta donned the battle apparel of the Drummonds. She had prepared for this day, and it had come. She felt stronger and powerful as she took up the scimitar and wielded it with ease. She would march alongside the mightiest warriors of all of Boltonia as well as Liam the human.

The newborn king was taken by Zarya to the Elders for protection. Garkov had returned safely and accompanied Zarya to the Rock Crystal Caves. It had been days since Astarta had seen her son. But it was for the best for the king, for Boltonia, and for her. She had to face the man she had loved and kill him. There was no room for error. It was now, on this day, for her to fulfill the prophecy.

They waited in the valley with the white-winged dragons in position for their purpose. Barsabbas and his allies held position from a vantage point in the White Mountains. They could see all that the Drummonds had.

As Astarta saw the first warrior come over the mountainside, she said, "The dragons should start flapping their wings."

"Dragons flap your wings," Prince Vella commanded the cyclops.

The white-winged dragons flapped their wings in simultaneous motion to create windstorms.

"What are you doing?" Liam asked Astarta.

"They can't hit what they can't see," Prince Vella said. "Haven't you learned anything here with us?"

"You both have to stay with me. He will not know it is me. He will have the Green Orb and will be using it. Both of you keep watch for that," Astarta instructed both Liam and Prince Vella. Then she kissed Vella on the cheek and Liam on the lips. She draped herself in her emerald-green cloak and tied her hood down tightly.

"This needs to be done now," she said.

The three marched into the storm.

"What is this? They are starting the storms before we get into the valley," Barrett declared as they reached the summit and saw the valley below them. "We have no way of knowing what is planned for us."

"Yes, we do. Randolf, what is the status?" Barsabbas asked.

Randolf went off into a vision.

He saw a boy leading the Drummond army. The boy marched up to Randolf and sliced his throat, which trapped Randolf in the vision, and he was left behind.

"My lord, you go into battle without a Merlinian?" Barrett asked.

"I have the Green Orb. I have no need for a Merlinian," Barsabbas said confidently as he directed his steed, Strength, down the mountainside and into the storm. "Make a pathway to those dragons. I will take care of those first."

Barrett raced ahead of Barsabbas and swung his sword back and forth, cutting through the crowd of Drummond warriors. The Merlinians' protection spell kept him from feeling the sharp pain of the cuts and gashes he received from the Drummond warriors' swords.

The Drummonds loaded large, flaming boulders onto the trebuchets and launched them. They hit their mark and took out a large platoon of Barsabbas's soldiers as they marched down the mountainside. The flames kept the rest of the army from ascending the mountain. This did not seem to faze Barsabbas, and he charged on, holding the Green Orb in his large right hand. He held out his left and touched all Drummonds in his path.

Astarta moved swiftly through the whipping sands, keeping a mental eye on both Prince Vella and Liam. She gave both a mental feeling of where she was going, and they followed without hesitation. She headed toward the mountains to stop Barsabbas before he managed more damage and destruction. She did not need her physical sight; she used her mental sight, following it until she was before Strength. Barsabbas charged by, missing her head with his left hand as he passed.

He is heading toward the dragons, Astarta thought at Liam and Vella.

Vella ran through the sands, swung his sword, and sliced through the right front and back legs of Strength. The massive rider crashed to the ground. The Green Orb was still fixed in the large right hand of Barsabbas as he struggled to stand. When he was upright, there stood before him a boy in a hooded cloak, the boy Randolf had spoken of from his vision.

"A boy? You send a boy?" Barsabbas yelled out to the battling warriors.

The boy before him swung his scimitar over his head and all around him.

The dragons received a mental command to stop flapping their wings, and the sandstorms subsided.

"I will not fight you, boy. I will just kill you," Barsabbas said as he reached out with his left hand. Before he could touch the boy, Liam sliced Barsabbas's hand off. Barsabbas did not cry out with the pain he felt. Vella approached Barsabbas and sliced off the other hand, which gripped the Green Orb. Barsabbas's eyes returned to their original colors immediately. Handless, Barsabbas stared at the boy who wielded the scimitar. Then the hood fell from the boy's head and revealed the strawberry-blonde hair of his love, Astarta. She took her scimitar and plunged it into the chest of the halfling she had once loved. As Barsabbas fell to his knees, the battle stopped around him.

"It is done, Astarta. You have destroyed me," Barsabbas said as he looked at his love. As he fell, she turned to walk away. "Astarta, I will love you always."

As Barsabbas fell to the ground and died, the hordes of soldiers and warriors cheered. Astarta called for Liam and Prince Vella, who had the Green Orb in his possession.

"You know what has to be done."

Chapter 17
There Will Be Peace

The three climbed the mountain to where Liam had found the Rock Crystal Caves to return the Green Orb to its rightful place. All the Elders greeted them and prepared a ceremony for the return of the Green Orb to its place upon the pedestal. The Elders gathered and performed a ritual, then preparing themselves with a ceremonial bath and a period of fasting. By the time they were done, the ground had been prepared for the ceremony with four shrines, one in each direction with elemental symbolism—air in the east, fire in the south, water in the west, the soil of the Drummond home in the north—and the pedestal at the center.

After the pedestal had been set up, the Elders lit the bonfire. Then the Elders sat and meditated. Nebo anointed Astarta, Liam, Prince Vella, Garkov, Zarya, and baby Auberon upon their foreheads and smudged them for purification using incense from a burning bundle of sage. They gathered in a circle.

The Elders began the ritual by sweeping the bounds of the circle. Then Nebo cleansed it with incense and cut the boundaries using the sacred athame. A brief invocation to the spirits of the four elements was offered at each shrine around the pedestal. Finally, the Elders faced one another and, standing between the bonfire and the pedestal, invoked the elements to become present in one another. They kissed one another, and each in turn spoke prophetic words to the gathered assembly.

Over the next hour, the community chanted, drummed, meditated, and danced to raise magikal energy for the Green Orb. Under the direction of Nebo, this energy was used to create a cone of power, which was then psychically directed to the power of the Green Orb. Nebo placed the Green Orb upon the pedestal. It began to glow, and the entire center room glowed green and became warm. A beam of green light shot out of the roof of the cave.

"It is now a time of peace," Nebo declared.

"What now?" Liam asked the Elder.

"Live," Nebo said. He walked away.

"We have a new king. We should rejoice and celebrate," Prince Vella said.

"Astarta," Nebo turned to the small group, "you must stay and continue your training."

"What of my son?" Astarta asked.

"He is not your son anymore. He is our king. Zarya will raise him and teach him the ways of the Drummond," Nebo said.

Astarta looked upon her son and kissed him. And after a long hug and many tears, she handed him off to Zarya.

"Do not worry, Lady Astarta, I will raise him as my own. He will be a strong and intelligent king," Zarya assured her as she took the child from Astarta.

"I am not worried about that, Zarya. I will miss him." Astarta kissed her son once more.

"Have you forgotten your teachings already, Astarta? You can see your son any time you wish," Nebo said.

"It will not be the same."

Garkov took Astarta's hand and patted it with her other.

"I will be there too, Lady Astarta," Garkov said.

"My good little Alrumes, you have been so loyal. Your duty is done. You can go home to the Haunted Forest."

"Lady Astarta, my duty is to you," Garkov told Astarta, smiling up at her.

Astarta moved over to Prince Vella.

"My protector, you have done well," she said. "I want you to assure me that my son will have the same protection you gave me."

"He will," Vella said as he bowed before her.

When he came upright again, he was met with a kiss. Then Astarta went to Liam, whose eyes were looking down. She lifted his head with her small, tender hand and kissed him.

"This is not good-bye. I will see you again. I pray to the Elders that your heart will still have me," she said, her voice strong even as tears fell from her eyes.

"It will take you in now and forever," Liam said as he kissed her again. Astarta did not want to let him go.

Astarta and Nebo watched as the group as they left the Rock Crystal Caves. As they exited the caves, they were met with snow falling all around them in the high elevation.

"This is good," Zarya said as she covered the baby king. Garkov danced in the newly fallen snow.

As they all looked over Boltonia, down below the mountain, it was raining. It was the first rain that Boltonia had seen since Barsabbas had stolen the Green Orb. The soldiers and warriors below looked up to the skies. They let the rain fall upon their bodies. Some yelled in celebration. Some danced to rejoice. Some stood with their mouths opened to taste the sweet liquid from the skies.

"Yes, all is good," Astarta agreed.

The cave entrance closed and stayed hidden.